Fifty
Spades
of Grey

Fifty
Spades
of Grey

BIG SKY PUBLISHING
www.bigskypublishing.com.au

L.O.L. James

Copyright © L.O.L James 2015

First published 2012
This edition 2015

Big Sky Publishing Pty Ltd
PO Box 303, Newport, NSW 2106, Australia
Phone: 1300 364 611
Fax: (61 2) 9918 2396
Email: info@bigskypublishing.com.au
Web: www.bigskypublishing.com.au

Cover design and typesetting: Think Productions
Author: James, L.O.L
Title: Fifty shades of grass / L.O.L James.
ISBN: 978-1-925275-07-0 (pbk.)
Series: James, L.O.L. Erotica for classy blokes; 3.
Subjects: Man-woman relationships--Fiction.

A CIP catalogue for this book is available from the British Library.

Printed and bound in Great Britain by
Marston Book Services Ltd, Oxfordshire

For Allie, the mistress of my universe,
who has a laugh like Sid James and loves a good
'Ooh err, missus' even more than I do.

Acknowledgements

I am indebted to the following people for their help and support:

My wife, Allie, thank you for tolerating my relentless bombardment of innuendo, you are my number one (fnarr fnarr).

Laura Robertson, for introducing me to *Viz Comics* and the delights of Finbarr Saunders.

'The Todd', from SCRUBS, give me an 'I'd Double Her Entendre' Five.

CSL, you make me smile whenever we meet.

Kenneth Williams, you will always be the king.

ELJ, when I think of you my breath hitches,
and I blush.

Denny and all the awesome team at BSP,
thank you for taking a punt.

Testimonials

"A nakedly cynical commercial rip off. The perfect stocking filler this Xmas."
– Nigel Marsh, Bestselling Author of *Fat, Forty and Fired* and the new *Fit, Fifty and Fired Up*

"This book is the perfect size for losing down the side of the couch."
– Cal Wilson, stand-up comedian, radio and television presenter

"If you look hard enough you can find the map of my life in these words."
– **Julia Morris, writer, comedian, actress and television presenter**

"Just like Fifty Shades, but well written."
– **A. Critic**

Christina was on her knees with both hands around the base, grunting loudly as she pulled with all her might.

Dave lightly touched her cheek with his long fingers. 'Let me help,' he offered. 'There's nothing worse than a pot-bound gardenia.'

Christina bit her lip and blushed deeply, her voice quivering as she softly asked, 'Does my bush bother you?'

'Don't be silly,' he reassured her running by his fingertips through it, sending a shiver down her body, 'I love viburnum.'

Christina's eyes widened in shock. She licked her lips and gushed, 'Oh my, what a huge bone. It's in so deep …'

'Yeah,' said Dave with a cheeky grin. 'Bloody spaniel buries them everywhere.'

He cradled Christina's head in his hands and whispered soothingly, 'You just lie back and relax and let me do some trimming.'

It was only fair after she'd done all the weeding, watering and mowing.

As Christina struggled through the door with her four large suitcases Dave said, 'I've been hard at it by myself while you've been away. Look, I've got calluses on my hands …'

She squealed with delight, realising Dave had finally got around to paving the garden path.

Christina held Dave by the shoulders. The desire and determined look in her eyes told him that she'd come to a decision. 'Tonight Dave I want it all. Give me your seed.'

'Geez, no worries. Relax,' he replied. 'I've already finished top dressing my lawn.'

She flushed bright red, coyly bit her lip then looked down and said, 'Summer is almost here, it's time to remove all that bushy stuff.'

'Absolutely, has to be done. As soon as it starts warming up everyone should rake last season's thatch off their lawn.'

'Wow, that's a nice, thick hose. It feels really solid in my hands,' Christina blurted out, giggling like a schoolgirl.

'They do cost a bit more,' he replied. 'But they're guaranteed not to kink and block the flow.'

'Arrghh! Please be a bit tender with my balls,' he screeched. 'They cost a fortune. You have to make sure the roots stay totally covered with soil when you pot annuals.'

Her voice was husky and pleading as she begged, 'Please, please, please. Just one root.'

'We can't, the green curry recipe says use the whole coriander plant. I don't know how you eat them raw anyway …'

Christina kissed him wetly on the chest, tracing a line up Dave's neck with her hot tongue, and then hissed into his ear, 'Doggy?'

'Ugh, no way,' Dave blurted out. 'Are you kidding? We spend enough time cleaning up after the bloody tabby.'

After three painful, sweaty hours of punishment Christina winced as she realised she had lost all the skin on her knees.

Dave looked down at her with tenderness and said, 'Look, I know they look a bit daggy, but please use the kneepads next time you want to weed the whole garden.'

She held Dave's hand and her deep brown eyes sparkled as she looked straight into his soul. 'Do you know how I'd like to use your pole?' she asked coyly.

Dave's breath hitched as he said, 'I'm not sure. Tomatoes? No wait, maybe runner beans?'

From up in the tree Christina wolf-whistled then called out in a teasing, mischievous tone, 'Hey handsome, from that angle you can probably see my honey pot.'

Dave laughed and said, 'Maybe, but I think the proper word for a bee home is "hive".'

'Squirt your thick cream all over my face,' Christina demanded, urgent desire obvious in her voice, 'and make sure it covers my lips.'

'Of course,' Dave agreed, slowly rubbing it in with his long fingers. 'On days like today, you gotta keep up the sunscreen.'

'Ho!' Dave shouted.

Christina looked stunned, 'I beg your pardon?'

'Sorry, I was off in my own world, how rude of me,' said Dave 'Could you pass me the hoe, please?'

'Oh … sure.'

A Little Too Filthy

Dave notices a strand of hair has come loose from Christina's ponytail and pushes it behind her ear.

Christina's breath hitches, then she blushes. 'Oh my,' she sighs, then bites her lip.

Dave sees her lip biting and quirks up his mouth.

Christina notices his quirking mouth and her breath hitches again.

Dave's breath hitches.

Christina blushes.

Dave blushes.

Christina is so flustered by the desire pooling deep inside her that she tries to bite her mouth that is quirking up, and mistakenly bites her tongue instead. 'Oh my,' she says as her inner goddess also hitches her breath and bites her lip.

As they lean in to kiss, Dave runs his long finger along her lip.

Her breath hitches again.

His mouth quirks up.

He puts his thumb in her mouth.

Christina explodes, 'Pee-yeuw! Where has that hand been?'

'Ahh, sorry,' says Dave. 'I've been spreading chook poo on your azaleas.'

'Holy crap,' she blurts out.

'Exactly,' he confirms.

Christina feels something that might potentially be described by a 16-year-old schoolgirl as a 'needy, achy discomfort' and wonders if it could be caused by desire, then realises it's being caused by the chook poo and starts to retch violently.

Dave notices that pesky strand of hair has come loose again but leaves it alone this time as he notices it has some bile on it.

Christina, still in her nightie, welcomed Dave at the door. 'Today I only have one thing planned for you, Mr Woode,' she purred dragging him inside. 'A nice ... long ... blow job.'

'Aww geez,' Dave sighed. 'Has that bloody Liquidambar tree dropped its leaves again?'

'I want to try something a little unusual,' Dave whispers into Christina's ear. 'I'm sure most people give it a go, but they don't really talk about it. It's just … I'll need you to tell me when it's the right time.'

'Yes, anything for you,' she purrs, feeling desire pool wetly in her body.

'I think we should try some blood and bone.'

'Wow, you saucy bugger. I'd love that.'

'Great,' said Dave, obviously relieved. 'Call me just when your roses are starting to wake up for spring and I'll go to the garden centre and pick some up.'

Christina and her best friend Kate were lounging around her pool when Dave called out from the flower beds, 'You ladies look bored, what if I went home and brought some of my best buds around to keep you occupied.'

Kate's ears pricked up and she grinned lasciviously, 'Sounds awesome.'

'Cool. My freesias are budding like mad. You may as well have some ...'

Dave was covered in sweat, leaning on the fence gulping down some water in the hot sun. Christina strolled up to him, casually playing with a long loop of soft rope.

'Hello, Mr Woode.'

'Ms Grey, whatever do you have planned for this afternoon?'

'I thought maybe I could work on some knots with you.'

'That'd be a great help,' said Dave. 'Then we can finish shellacking the other woodwork.'

'Dave …' Christina murmured quietly, gathering up courage, 'I think we've been working together for long enough, I thought maybe we could talk about trying … how can I put it … golden showers?'

Dave shrugged, 'Just get a couple of five-buck sprinklers and you'll be fine.'

Christina walked in with her mobile, 'That was Kate, she was thinking of coming around tonight.' Christina's mouth had quirked up into a cheeky grin 'She's got some Spanish Fly.'

'Tell her not to worry,' said Dave. 'I'll give her some of those citronella candles.'

Christina walked away muttering, 'I wish you'd wet your wick.'

'When I'm outside here with you, in the privacy of my own garden,' cooed Christina as she cuddled up to Dave on the sun bed, 'I think I could get quite anal.'

'Me too,' said Dave giving her a squeeze. 'Even though I'm an Aussie, and love things a bit wild, I have to admit I prefer a formal garden.'

'Do you know Dave, I think you're a bit bi-curious,' Christina said out of nowhere.

'Sure, who isn't?' replied Dave, not even slightly perturbed.

She went on, 'Have you ever tried a bit of bi?'

'Of course,' Dave smiled at the memory. 'It adds variety and mixes things up. You get stems and leaves in the first season, then flowers in the next. Who wouldn't like biennials?'

Dave leaned in and asked tenderly, 'How would you like your bed?'

'I don't care,' said Christina as her breath hitched. 'I'd do it here on the grass.'

'My dear girl, I can't plant my rhubarb here on the grass,' laughed Dave.

She sighed, 'That's what you think.'

Christina had her face down in the grass, cursing and growling with the intense effort, 'I want it all, keep trying. Please … don't stop … I. Want. It. ALL!'

'Let's stop. It's no good …' said Dave, putting his hand on her shoulder softly. 'We'll use some weed killer. Sometimes you just can't get the whole taproot.'

Christina had a sensuous tone to her voice as she called out, 'Come into the kitchen, Dave. I'm ready to toss your salad.'

'Give me five minutes,' he called back. 'I'm almost finished planting your next crop of watercress and rocket.'

'Oh Dave, I'm so disappointed,' sighed Christina. 'You promised I'd get nine inches last night.'

'I'm sorry,' he replied sheepishly. 'The weatherman swore it would snow.'

Christina was lying back on a blanket as Dave was doing some clipping.

She giggled and said, 'I thought I'd try some … ahh … topiary?' She bit her lip and winked at Dave. 'What do you think? A brazilian? A landing strip?'

He thought for a minute before coming to a decision, 'To be honest, I reckon you can't go passed the fun hedges like a bunny, or a teddy bear.'

'I bought some chains,' Christina announced showing Dave her bag from the hardware store.

'What for?' he asked.

'That's for you to guess.' 'No … you don't mean …'

'I do.'

'Really?'

'Let's do it.'

'You're a legend!' Dave exploded and hugged Christina tightly, jumping up and down with excitement. 'Our own PORCH SWING. Awesome. My Gran used to have one, I LOVE those things.'

'Oh my … it's not every day you catch a man pitching a little tent in his shorts,' laughed Christina.

'Holy crap. Sorry darl,' said Dave, standing up showing it off. 'I've put up that toy Wiggle's tepee for your niece, but you're right, I shouldn't be walking around in just my Stubbies when she gets here. I'll put my shirt back on.'

'Servant, come here,' barked Christina as she loudly whipped something through the air. 'Mistress has bought a few lengths of nice, stiff cane.'

'Sorry Mistress,' said Dave, 'but you'll need a lot more than that to screen off that whole shed.'

'Kate and I need you to settle a bet, Dave,' Christina said laughingly as Dave walked inside.

'What is it this time?' Dave replied looking slightly troubled, knowing this could lead anywhere.

'Okay. What type of man are you - cut or uncut?' asked Kate.

'Ahh, that's easy,' he said relaxing. 'I always like my roses long-stemmed.'

'Wow, your tulips are a beautiful pink,' Dave said pointing at them.

'And you should be looking somewhere else when the wind blows up my skirt,' Christina laughed.

Christina was husky, urgent, and even desperate.
'I want to try a collar. Can we try a collar?'

'Of course, my love,' replied Dave, gently tussling
her hair. 'But I guarantee your cat won't like it.'

Kate and Christina were sitting back in deck chairs, drinking Bollinger, watching Dave and his mate José working. 'Keep it up, lads,' Kate cheered. 'Nothing better than seeing men mowing a lawn in thongs.'

'No problems,' laughed Dave. 'You ladies can keep your Havianas. José and I will stick with the good old K-Mart double-pluggers!'

'Dave, you cheeky thing,' teased Christina.
'My neighbour said she caught you sitting up in my
tree using binoculars trying to look at her nest.'

'So what? I'm only human. It was gorgeous,'
Dave protested. 'I've been watching three eggs
in there for ages, and today the chicks hatched!
It was beautiful ...'

Dave walked up to Christina who was lying on a sun bed under an umbrella, looking intensely at her laptop. 'You look very serious. What are you looking at?' he asked.

'Oh it's all so confusing. Things are going well between us, so I'm going to buy a cap. I'm trying to work out the right size.'

'Oh, yuck. I don't want to know about caps,' Dave cringed.

'Well it affects you too,' Christina said.

'I know it does, I have to be seen out with you.'

'What ARE you talking about?'

'Bloody American baseball caps. What's wrong with a good old Aussie Akubra? Or a Greg Chappell cricket hat?'

'Things are moving into new and … ah …
interesting areas for us, Dave,' Christina said,
blushing slightly and biting her lip. 'If we're going to
go to the next level, I think we should both say what
we would lay down as our hard limits?'

Dave nodded, 'Sure. Well for me, I think on this
level I'd use pavers, but on the veggie patch up the
back I'd lay down some railway sleepers. Give it a
nice rustic feel!'

Christina was straddling Dave as he lay down on a bench at the back of her garden. She flashed him a decadent smile and hissed, 'You just lie there, I'm going to pop inside to get a bottle of baby oil then come out here and go crazy.'

'I'm not sure darling,' replied Dave. 'I think for outdoor furniture you're meant to use teak oil.'

'Oh Dave,' laughed Christina, 'Kate will be here soon, let's put those bulbs away.'

'How long do we have?' Dave asked 'There's only another 50 or so daffodils to plant.'

'No, I meant your shorts are a bit tight for polite company,' giggled Christina. 'I can see your nuts.'

'I can see you're nuts if you think Kate is polite company,' Dave replied.

'Christina? Have you ever tried a few Lebanese cucumbers?' asked Dave, looking up from the veggie patch.

'Nah,' she replied. 'I once kissed a Lebanese guy, but it didn't go that far …'

Christina and her friend Kate were whispering about something as they shared a glass of Pouilly Fumé on the terrace.

'Dave?' Kate started.

But Christina choked on her wine and hushed her saying, 'Holy crap, Kate. You can't ask him …'

Kate ignored her friend and went on, 'Do you like a woman who spits or swallows?'

'Ahhh …' Dave mumbled, looking at Christina, 'can I answer?'

Christina looked sheepish but said, 'Go on.'

'I don't really go for wine tastings. More a beer man,' Dave shrugged.

Christina walked up behind Dave, suddenly grabbed him by the hair and whispered into his ear, 'You. Are. My. SLAVE.'

'No,' Dave replied. 'I. Am. Your. Gardener.'

'I'm slightly embarrassed,' Christina babbled out over a third glass of Sancerre, 'so I'm just going to say this. Dave … ahh … I … ahh … I want to give you my backdoor cherry.'

'It's a bit late for that isn't it?' scoffed Dave.

'Holy crap. How dare you? What do you mean?' Christina flushed deep red.

'Your English Morello by the backdoor, it looks pretty well established where it is. If you moved it you'd kill it.'

'Dave, come here. Now!' Christina was insistent. 'I want you to play with my beaver.'

Roaring with laughter Dave said, 'Hah! You're in Australia now, not Canada. Those furry things in the trees are called "possums".'

Forever In My Bed

'Christina!' Dave called from the garden.

'I'm still in my pyjamas, want to come inside?'
she answered.

'But I'm all dirty,' he called out.

'Well, in that case,' Christina giggled, 'just poke
your head through my back door.'

'Hi,' Dave said with a big smile. 'I'm sorting out the
flower beds. What type of peony do you like?'

'The mood I'm in today, I'll take whatever peony
I can get my hands on.'

'Seriously.'

'What type of peony do think would suit my bed?'

'Well,' said Dave, 'there's a single peony, like the
Krinkled White …'

'I don't think I could ever be satisfied with a just
single peony, especially not a krinkled white one.'

'Okay, there's a type called semi-double, there's a double peony …'

'I like the sound of a double peony.'

'Sure, I think you could handle a double peony.'

'Mmm, me too. Perhaps you and José could give me a double peony?'

'Great, and I'm thinking a fragrant one?'

'Of course, I adore a strongly scented peony.'

'Great, but there are still loads to choose from,' Dave said reading from a battered old garden book. 'Bandit … Baroness Schroeder … Pink Parfait … Now this one sounds good, "Pink Parfait is a fragrant, double peony of rich, dark pink".'

'Whatever Dave, you choose,' purred Christina. 'As long as I know I'm going to wake up every day with a "fragrant pink double peony" in my bed.'

'Do you think our relationship could handle swinging?' said Christina, biting her lip, a wicked flash in her deep, brown eyes.

'I think we could handle it. It'd be fun,' said Dave. 'But a swing set would totally ruin your begonias.'

'Help me, Dave … I feel so … dirty. Help me, please.'

'Sure,' said Dave, as he turned around and threw a bucket of water on her. 'There you go, all clean.'

Dave answered his ringing phone, 'Mr Woode? It's me,' said Christina slowly, trying not to sound drunk.

'Hello there, Ms Grey,' he chuckled. 'By the sound of your voice, you and Kate have had a great afternoon.'

'I can hear down the phone that you are smiling like a Cheshire cat at the thought of me being ever-so-tipsy?' mumbled Christina, dropping all pretence.

'Ah, no … That's last night's curry repeating on me. Sorry.'

'No problem, my handsome man. I'm ringing because Kate has a suggestion for us. The weather is getting colder, and she has given me a brilliant idea for something we could try to keep things hot through winter, if you get what I mean,' she slurred.

'Okay …' Dave said hesitantly, not sounding totally convinced.

'Don't be like that,' purred Christina. 'I've been reading about it on the Internet, and it sounds worth trying. Have you ever had a go at felching?'

Dave shrugged, 'Wood chips and straw and stuff around a plant? Of course, it works a treat over a really dry summer too.'

'You know what I've always wanted to try out here in my garden?' asked Christina as she scratched her fingernails down Dave's chest, leaving welt marks on his skin.

'No,' said Dave, as his mouth quirked up into a smile. 'What would you like in your garden, Ms Grey?'

'Froggy style.'

'Really?' Dave raised an eyebrow, genuinely surprised. 'I would never have picked that. I thought your taste in a manicured garden would be more English than French.'

'Kate told me about something called tea-bagging,' declared Christina, trying to sound nonchalant.

'Yes, I think we should do it,' Dave replied.

'Really? Oh my,' Christina said breathily.

'Yeah, fresh tea leaves, teabags, roses love 'em all.'

Christina walked outside rubbing her eyes and Dave stood up, clapping his hands together enthusiastically. 'Good morning. I hope you're feeling energetic today because I'd really like to touch up your water feature.'

'Wow,' laughed Christina, 'tell me more, kind sir …'

'Well it's been leaking non-stop for years …' continued Dave, 'so I thought I'd really dive in and get that licked, then give it a good coat of whitewash.'

Christina was watching the muscles in Dave's back flex as he rolled new turf onto her lawn. 'It wouldn't take long for a man like you to really have me squirting,' she called out seductively.

Dave stood up and considered her words. 'Well, you could do it by hand but for a lawn this size I'd use a sprinkler.'

'You look tired,' said Christina trying to distract her man. 'How about you come over here and feel my melons.'

'If you like,' he replied. 'But my mum reckons the best way to tell if they're ripe is to smell 'em.'

'Please. Now. Do it!' she said shaking with anticipation. 'Oh for goodness sake shove it in. Ram it home NOW!'

Dave grinned, 'Whoa there. I know we're almost done for the day and your "G&T" is calling, but gently does it with sensitive plants like rhododendrons.'

'Oh my, Dave. All day long, I've been thinking of having a bit of rough outside,' Christina said slyly.

'Finally a decision,' Dave replied, obviously relieved. 'So you're definitely going with a cobblestone path? Great choice.'

Christina had a glazed, faraway look in her eyes. 'Oh my. It's soft, yet firm at the same time. So swollen and full, and look how veiny it is underneath …'

'Awesome, isn't it? Not much to look at, but it feels lovely on your skin, and there's so many other uses for Aloe Vera too,' Dave responded.

Christina was lying on the sun bed watching the sun go down. 'Oh Dave, what does a girl have to do to get a shag in her garden?'

'Move,' he said bluntly.

'What?' she replied, confused.

Dave explained. 'Well, you're a bit far from the sea for cormorants. You'd have to move closer to the beach.'

'Stick around after work tonight, Dave,' she said with a wicked look on her face. 'I'll make you dinner and then we can jump in the sack.'

'Woohoo!' Dave shouted. 'Love it. Then what about a good old-fashioned egg 'n' spoon race?'

Giving him a sly sideways glance, she asked, 'Dave, could you show me the right way to do spooning?'

He replied, 'No need. When you're fertilising a veggie patch this big you can just chuck in handfuls.'

Christina walked in with a brown paper shopping bag. She seemed nervous, biting her lip. Then her breath hitched as she seemed to find courage, 'Dave, would you try out a ball gag on me?'

'Sure … ahh … if it's what you really want?'

She bit her lip again, but seemed determined, 'I do, Dave, I do.'

Dave seemed unsure, but then grinned and said, 'Did you hear the one about the bloke with three knackers?'

'Are you coming inside for dinner?' Christina called out, 'I've been waiting all day to get my mouth around your plums.'

Dave just rolled his eyes and said, 'You didn't have to wait. They fell off your tree so they're yours.'

'Did you see that huge wet spot we left last night?' asked Christina with a smirk.

'Ahh, don't' worry,' Dave said, giving her a squeeze and kissing her forehead. 'It looks pretty mucky, but new grass loves a good soaking.'

'Dave, I'm furious with you,' Christina stormed in, boiling with rage. 'Kate told me about you coming across her butt.'

'I ... ahh ...' Dave stammered.

'Is it true?'

'Yes.'

'You bastard. Were you going to tell me?'

'Look, it was only once and ...'

'Only once!'

'Look, she's trying really hard to give up smoking. I came across one cigarette butt in the gazanias. She swore it won't happen again.'

Christina was rubbing her hands together, 'Time for a nice, big serve of your special cream.'

'Sure, that mower was pretty greasy wasn't it?' Dave replied. 'Don't worry, this hand wash does the trick.'

Wearing nothing but a very small bikini, Christina strode outside and stood over Dave. 'Right Mr Woode. It's midday. Time for a break. Maybe today you'd like to go downtown.'

'Thanks but no time, sorry. I've brought a few sangas anyway,' Dave said without looking up.

An urgent, pleading tone was in Christina's voice. Her breath hitched, she bit her lip and whispered into his neck, 'Oh Dave, I want your fingers all over my little rosebud.'

'Not a great idea, sorry. They're pretty sensitive. In fact, most species – particularly ones like your Centifolia rose – prefer to be left alone when they're just budding. Did you know that most of the "Old Garden Roses" as the Centifolia are called, are known to be … Christina … where are you going?'

'I'm sure you're tired after a hard day's work but
I really need you to stay over and plow away for
me all night long,' Christina pouted like a schoolgirl.

'What? No way,' Dave dismissed the idea.
'Sorry, but I've already put in a good ten hour day.
I can finish the veggie garden tomorrow.'

Whatever Did You Have in Mind?

'Hi Dave,' Christina smiled lewdly as she spoke into the phone. She then covered the receiver, turned to her friend Kate and put her finger to her lip doing the 'shoosh' signal. 'What? Oh nothing. It's just, my dearest, dearest friend Kate is here ...'

'Ahhh,' said Dave, knowing this could lead anywhere.

'Don't be like that,' Christina said.

'Hi Dave,' Kate shouted out.

'Well,' Dave went on, 'she can be a bit naughty can't she?'

Christina pretended to be horrified, 'Naughty? Never!'

'Anyway, what is it you ladies had in mind?' asked Dave.

'Well, we were having a few glasses of Pouilly Fumé ...'

'Yes,' said Dave sounding ever more doubtful.

'And we were wondering …'

'Yes …'

'If you and that friend of yours, José might want to come around?'

'Sure,' said Dave. 'What did you have in mind?'

Christina's breath hitched and Kate bit her lip. She gave Kate a huge, sly grin to indicate Dave seemed keen, then went on, 'Oh, nothing specific. We thought maybe we might have a few drinks, get a bit silly, then maybe we could all …'

'Yes?'

'Ahh … finish off by making a daisy chain.'

'Oh bloody hell Christina.'

'What?'

Dave let out a very annoyed sigh, 'Hang up. I've got a phone call to make.'

'To José?' Christina asked.

Dave grumbled, 'No, Little Miss Daisy Chain, the garden centre. I wish you'd make up your mind, I just ordered six dozen tulips.'

'If you want to be the pitcher,' she hissed bawdily in Dave's ear, 'I would happily be the catcher.'

He thought for a second and then said, 'I think we should leave the new lawn for a fortnight or so before we play any sports on it.'

'Hey Dave,' Kate called out. 'Christina's neighbour just looked over the fence and said we had great tits.'

'Nah, he's wrong!' said Dave.

'How dare you?' the girls said together, shocked.

'Calm down, we don't have them in Australia,' Dave chuckled. 'If they were black and white you probably saw baby magpies or willy wagtails.'

Kate and Christina were sharing a bottle of Bollinger on the terrace, soaking up the sun watching Dave work.

'Dave, my love, can you help Kate and I?' Christina called out. 'We desperately need someone to rub sunscreen on our hooters.'

Dave strode over and said, 'Sure. My hands are all yours ladies.'

He squirted a big glob of cream on each hand and said, 'Lie back and close your eyes.'

Then he wiped an index finger on each of their noses. Both girls screeched in surprise.

'There you go,' he announced, walking away. 'Sunscreen on your lovely hooters.'

She hissed fiercely at him, 'Look at my gash now. Look at it. It's dripping God dammit.'

'I'm sorry Christina,' Dave replied calmly. 'Don't think I'm insensitive, but it's hardly a gash, just a very small cut, but ...' Dave switched to a condescending baby voice, 'If Kwistina wike it, I put a bandaid on your ouchie.'

'Kate's coming around for dinner tonight. We've got something special planned; Christina announced. 'I hope you like the taste of poontang.'

'I'm sorry but I don't; Dave cringed. 'I love a green or red curry though? Maybe a Pad Thai?'

'Up there!' The girls were pointing into the top of the big gum.

'What is it?' Dave asked.

'Look up there. Kate's seen a cockatoo,' Christina shrieked.

'I have no doubt,' Dave said only half under his breath. 'And then some …'

'Phew. That's a pretty impressive package,' Christina exclaimed, her eyes bulging as she flushed a deep red.

'Yeah, it arrived today,' said Dave. '200 crocus bulbs; all yours.'

'Now that we're outside …' she began, touching her finger on his lips. 'I want to try dogging?'

'I can't win,' Dave retorted irritably.

Christina looked shocked at his response.

He went on, 'Well, make up your mind. Last week you told me right off for peeing on a tree, now you want to try it.'

Christina was sidling up to Dave on their rug, rubbing her body against him. She kissed his belly button and licked his stomach, 'I feel like wrapping my luscious lips around a nice, meaty pair of cojones.'

'Now there's a thought,' said Dave with a hungry grin. 'If you're going Mexican I'd love a couple of burritos.'

'Oooh Dave, my bottom is so sore. Can we try the front?' moaned Christina.

'Sure,' he replied, kissing her shoulder. 'Let's get off this stone wall and go round to the seats on the front porch.'

'Are you okay? You look like you're in pain?' asked Dave gently, leaning in and kissing Christina's cheek.

'This is a bit embarrassing,' murmured Christina, 'but I'm having some trouble with my grapes.'

'Oh, sorry,' muttered Dave. 'I'll get some clippers and trim them off.'

Christina sparked up with a wicked smile, 'Kate and I noticed you admiring our jugs.'

'Of course. They're beautiful,' Dave agreed. 'I love using old kitchen stuff as flower pots, jugs, teapots, watering cans; they look classy and quaint.'

'Arrggh Daaaave,' Christina groaned.

'I'm just going to come out and say it,' Christina announced. 'I want to try some anal.'

'Ahh,' Dave looked unsure, and a bit embarrassed 'I'm pretty sure you pronounce that word "an – nu – al".'

'Hello?' answered Dave.

'Hi Dave, it's me,' Christina said into the phone. 'I want to see you tonight. I want you to come on over and let's do it like rabbits.'

'You're kidding, aren't you?' replied Dave curtly. 'We've worked on that garden for three weeks now. I'm not going to dig up the grass and then shit everywhere?'

Christina walked out to the bottom of her back garden and sat down next to Dave.

'I want a deck.'

'You want a deck?'

'Where?'

'I want a deck, here in the bottom.'

'How big?'

'When it comes to a deck, I think the bigger the better.'

'Careful, you probably don't have as much room round the back for a deck as you do in the front.'

'I've got enough room round the back, I could fit a pretty large deck.'

'I can do that for you.'

'You can give me the decking I'm after?'

'How deep do you want it?'

'If it's a big deck, it'll be nice and deep won't it?'

'No doubt. And I am just the man to give you some nice deep decking.'

'I'd love some nice long decking from you.'

'Hardwood.'

'Of course.'

Christina bit her lip and blushed a deep red, 'Crap. Double crap. Holy crap.'

'Yep,' Dave said sulkily. 'That bloody cat shits everywhere.'

Rare And Beautiful

'Dave, I'm glad you're here,' Christina called out, digging her friend Kate in the ribs. 'I was just about to tell Kate our fantastic news.'

'Hi Kate,' said Dave. 'Yeah, great news. I was having a bit of a poke around between Christina's lobelia.'

Kate started giggling, 'You what?'

'Yesterday I was tidying up Christina's lobelia – they were right out of control, all over the place …' said Dave.

The girls looked at each other and both said, 'Oh my,' and then giggled uproariously.

Dave went on unperturbed, 'Anyway … I was having a look in between two of Christina's lobelia and, when I parted them with my fingers, I found a clitoria.'

Kate and Christina erupted with laughter.

Christina spoke between giggles, 'It's apparently a clitoria fragrans, a very rare flower.'

'This is serious,' protested Dave. 'I've never heard of them in this country.'

'It's wonderful you've discovered my clitoria, Dave,' Christina said in mock seriousness. 'And I look forward to having you tend it for me as often as possible.'

Dave turned to Kate, 'I'll bet you've never even seen a clitoria before?'

'Of course I have,' guffawed Kate. 'Every morning.'

'What? Do you have one too?'

'Of course, I have a beautiful pink clitoria.'

'No way.'

'Yes.'

Dave was stunned 'The clitoria macrophylla! Get outta town! That's even more rare.'

Kate went on, 'It's very sensitive.'

'I'm sure it is,' said Dave. 'You'd have to really look after it.'

'I gently give it a once over almost every single day, my lad.'

'Could I see it?'

'Well, mine is hidden behind a bush too.'

'I'd love to see it.'

'Sure,' said Kate, unbuttoning her jeans.

'Okay, that's enough,' said Christina.

'I can't help noticing how long your fingers are,' Christina blurted out, taking Dave by surprise. 'And you know what they say about extra-large fingers ...'

'Yep,' grinned Dave. 'Extra-large gardening gloves!'

'Take my flower,' hissed Christina.

Dave gritted his teeth and hissed back, 'Take it yourself, I'm carrying three bags of potting mix.'

'I haven't gone near it for a month, so it was a bit stiff this morning, but a couple of quick pulls and off it goes,' Dave beamed with pride.

'Thanks Dave,' Christina was grinning from ear to ear. 'So now I just go up and down with it?'

'Yep.'

'I hope the neighbours don't mind the noise,' she added.

Dave shook his head. 'Don't worry, you'll be finished mowing the lawn in no time.'

'Bring those gorgeous long fingers over here,' purred Christina with a knowing smile on her face. 'I need them in my hole.'

Dave rolled his eyes, 'Have you lost that necklace down the drain again?'

'If we're going to do this, I think we should agree on a "safe word", Christina suggested.

'Sure,' agreed Dave. 'When I was a kid it was always "bar" or "home".'

'Now the garden is finished,' Christina said softly, obviously struggling to say what she was thinking, 'perhaps you and José could come around … you know, together … and we could … ahhh, have a spit roast?'

'Wow. Are you kidding?' Dave almost shouted with excitement. 'I'm not sure the three of us could finish off a whole lamb.'

'I want you to be my sub,' Christina demanded, licking her lips with anticipation.

'Okay,' said Dave. 'And when we're finished that, I want you to be my fire engine.'

Kate and Christina were sitting on the lawn in their bikinis. Christina looked down and said, 'Oh Dave, I'm not sure I like my bush totally bald …'

'Don't worry, it'll grow back,' Dave said soothingly. 'Clematis always gets a little woody over winter. Have you thought about getting an evergreen like star jasmine or gardenia? They have nice, big bush with splashes of white and smell gorgeous.'

Kate almost choked on her glass of wine, 'Does he really not realise when he says those things.'

'No,' Christina said with a sigh and a smile.

Dave shook his head and walked away muttering, 'Aww, forget it you two. I'll go back to spraying my fertiliser on your asters.'

The girls burst out laughing.

'Can you handle some pain?' she asked.

'Sure, I'm tough,' he said.

'But are you willing to suffer for me?'

'Sure.'

'Are you ready to endure the most pain any man alive can go through?'

'Yes,' he answered with conviction.

'Then read this, cover to cover,' Christina said as she handed him a book with a grey necktie on the front.

'You just missed José,' Kate said as Dave arrived.

Dave laughed, 'He's been around a lot lately. Is that to see you, Kate?'

'He didn't have a mower,' Christina answered for her. 'He said something about cutting your grass,' she added cheekily.

'Did he?' asked Dave with a laugh. 'Well, the lawn could use some good forking.'

'Good morning, Dave,' chirped Christina.
'You're here early.'

'I thought I'd get all my work done today,' replied Dave, 'so I could finish the day by getting stuck into your date.'

'I'll drink to that,' she said with a wicked grin, raising her morning coffee in a cheers.

'Once I've got it trimmed and looking good,' Dave went on, 'I'll plant it next to your Christmas palm out the back to make a pair.'

Christina smiled. 'I do like a pair of palms in my back passage.'

'Bloody neighbours!' muttered Christina under her breath.

'What's the problem?' asked Dave, putting his arm around her shoulder.

'Their 16-year-old son is always banging his balls against my fence,' she said. 'And their bloody dog … he digs up the lawn, knocks over my bins, but to be honest it's his poo I find hard to swallow.'

'No doubt,' laughed Dave, then winced as he got an elbow in the ribs.

About the Author

Since early childhood L.O.L. James (the obvious pseudonym) dreamed of writing crass double entendres that readers would find stupid and offensive – then titter in spite of their good taste, but he put those dreams on hold to focus on his career and family. He finally hardened up (see, he can't help himself!) and put pen to paper with a series that pays homage to another series which began paying homage to an even earlier series.

At present he is the author of the smutty, garden-themed, *Fifty Spades of Grey,* the offensively sporting *Fifty Shades of Grass* and the blatantly obscene DIY collection, *Fifty Shelves of Grey.*

Of course, like all authors in the romance genre, if there's a buck to be made he'll happily write another book – even if some characters have to be brought back from the dead by having them apparently have a 'secret twin brother' return from years spent in a small monastery in Nepal.

L.O.L. James is a husband and father of three based in Eastern Sydney who is, frankly, slightly embarrassed that his kids might read this one day.

Also Available

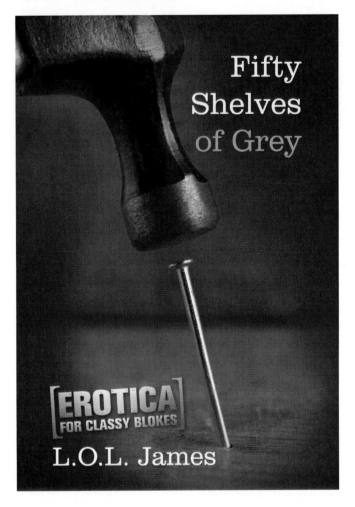

Fifty
Shelves
of Grey

[EROTICA]
FOR CLASSY BLOKES

L.O.L. James

Christina is attempting to use the jargon of home DIY to speak the language of love. Dave, totally unaware of her efforts, just thinks he's finally found someone as passionate about nailing, screwing and the importance of using the right lubricant when you're working away on someone's back door.

Fifty
Shades
of Grass

[EROTICA]
FOR CLASSY BLOKES

L.O.L. James

Christina tries to use Dave's love of sport to get him into bed, but of course he has no clue and is just 'stoked' he's found a girl who adores talking about bouncers, behinds, and superb ball handling as much as he does.